DAVID COVERDALE
A Life In Vision

DAVID COVERDALE
A Life In Vision

Andy Francis

WYMER
PUBLISHING
Bedford, England

First published in Great Britain in 2019
by Wymer Publishing
www.wymerpublishing.co.uk
Tel: 01234 326691
Wymer Publishing is a trading name of Wymer (UK) Ltd

Copyright © 2019 Wymer Publishing.
This edition © 2022

ISBN: 978-1-912782-00-4

The Author hereby asserts his rights to be identified
as the author of this work in accordance with sections
77 to 78 of the Copyright, Designs & Patents Act 1988.

All rights reserved. No part of this publication may be
reproduced or transmitted in any form or by any means,
electronic or mechanical, including photocopying, or any
information storage and retrieval system, without written
permission from the publisher.

This publication is sold subject to the condition that it shall not,
by way of trade or otherwise, be lent, re-sold, hired out or
otherwise circulated without the publishers prior consent in any
form of binding or cover other than that in which it is published
and without a similar condition including this condition
being imposed on the subsequent purchaser.

Every effort has been made to trace the copyright holders of the
photographs in this book but some were unreachable. We would
be grateful if the photographers concerned would contact us.

Design by Andy Bishop / 1016 Sarpsborg
Printed and bound by Harrier LLC, England.

A catalogue record for this book is available from the British Library.

Madison Square Garden, New York, USA, 9th October 1980.

© Bill O'Leary

The Early Years

David Coverdale was born on 22nd September 1951, in Saltburn-by-the-Sea, North Yorkshire. By 1967 he began performing briefly with the aptly named, Vintage 67, before moving on to Denver Mule, formed with a few friends he had met at school and the Green Lane Art College in Middlesborough that he was then attending. The following year they called it a day, and he was soon picked to join The Skyliners, a band that had established in 1963. Shortly after David joined, the band changed its name to The Government with whom he was with between 1968-72.

In these early days David spent many an evening at the Redcar Jazz Club, which despite its name, played host to most of the top names from the world of rock and pop through the sixties and early seventies. Indeed, whilst a member of The Skyliners, they supported Joe Cocker & The Grease Band at only his second gig.

Graham Lowe was the resident photographer at the Jazz Club and his girlfriend used to sell photos at the Picture Gallery to those who frequented the club. "How many I sold I can't remember", as he recalled many years later, "but the odd ten bob was pretty good. I even sold one to Dave Coverdale."

As with any jobbing band of the day The Government took whatever gigs they could. This saw them mixing cabaret shows where they performed material such as The Beatles 'Yesterday' and Scott Walker's 'Joanna', and more straightforward rock shows where their set included covers from the top rock acts of the day such as T. Rex, Black Sabbath ('Paranoid') and ironically, Deep

Purple ('Hush' & 'Black Night'). Roger Baker, The secretary of The Jazz Club and the band's manager takes the credit for this. "I actually spent some time persuading them to sing current hit numbers. He sang a few pop numbers and the group did marvellously well."

David even found himself supporting Deep Purple at a show at Bradford University in 1969. By all accounts, Purple's Jon Lord and Roger Glover were suitably impressed as they watched the band' soundcheck, which included a version of the Johnny Kidd hit 'Shakin' All Over'. As Purple had only recently changed line-up, Jon Lord took David's number, in case new vocalist Ian Gillan didn't work out, but after a few weeks he gave up hope of receiving a call.

By 1971 the band made their first recording on 20th February at Multicord Studios in Sunderland. They recorded four tracks, 'The Letter', 'Bang Bang' (By Sonny Bono), Bobby Womack's 'It's All Over Now' and 'Does Anybody Know What Time It Is?' which had been on the debut album by Chicago Transit Authority in 1969.

But shortly after, The Government cut its workload back to weekend gigs, allowing them to focus on day jobs as well. David briefly took a gig with a band called Harvest for a tour of Denmark, but on returning to Redcar he got a salesman's job working at an offshoot of the Gentry Boutique called Stride in Style.

During this period he gigged with Rivers Invitation. Along with a couple of the other band members he was also part of the house band at the town's Starlite Club, while selling clothes during the day.

| DOZY, BEAKY, MICK AND TICH SATURDAY, 28th FEBRUARY PLUS THE GOVERMENT From 8 p.m. to 11.45 p.m. ADMISSION 10/- | SUNDAY, 1st March THE GOVERMENT PLUS ALL THE TOP TEN RECORDS From 8 p.m. to 11.45 p.m. ADMISSION FREE | VIKING BALLROOM SEAHOUSES Tel. 628 |

LATE TRAINS FROM REDCAR (Sunday) Last train to M'bro', Thornaby and Darlington 11-08 ; Marske and Saltburn 11-06.
CLUB DANCES When late transport is arranged by the Club it is essential that bus tickets be purchased before 10 p.m. It is a condition of a late licence bar that ticket holders only be allowed in a dance after 10-30 p.m. No Pass Outs after 10 p.m.
CAR PARKING Cars may be parked without lights on the seaward side of Promenade. No Parking behind Coatham Hotel.

FUTURE ATTRACTIONS

Sunday, Nov. 5th—**AMAZING BLONDEL** .... Plus — Prelude
Sunday, Nov. 12th—**ROXY MUSIC** .... Plus — Khan
Sunday, Nov. 19th—**SANDY DENNY** .... Plus — Hedgehog Pie
Sunday, Nov. 26th—**CURVED AIR** .... Plus — Graphite
Sunday, Dec. 3rd—**ARTHUR BROWN'S KINGDOM COME** .... Plus — Brave New World
Sunday, Dec. 10th—**STACKRIDGE** .... Plus — 25 Views of Worthing
Sunday, Dec. 17th—**MANN** .... Plus — Back Door
Sunday, Dec. 24th—**J.S.D. BAND** .... Plus — Government
Sunday, Dec. 31st—**HACKENSACK** .... Plus — Toss-Ta

All programmes are subject to alteration and the committee cannot be responsible for the non-appearance of Artists.

| A " SOUND " INVESTMENT **'GOVERNMENT'** Management : 6 WEST END, GUISBOROUGH Tel. Guisborough 2504 | **ECONOMY CAR SALES** GOOD SELECTION OF USED CARS ALWAYS AVAILABLE LORD ST., REDCAR Tel. Redcar 71056 |

MARSKE WORKINGMEN'S CLUB

SATURDAY, MAY 27th

GOVERNMENT

SHOW BAND GROUP

Members and bona-fide guests welcome

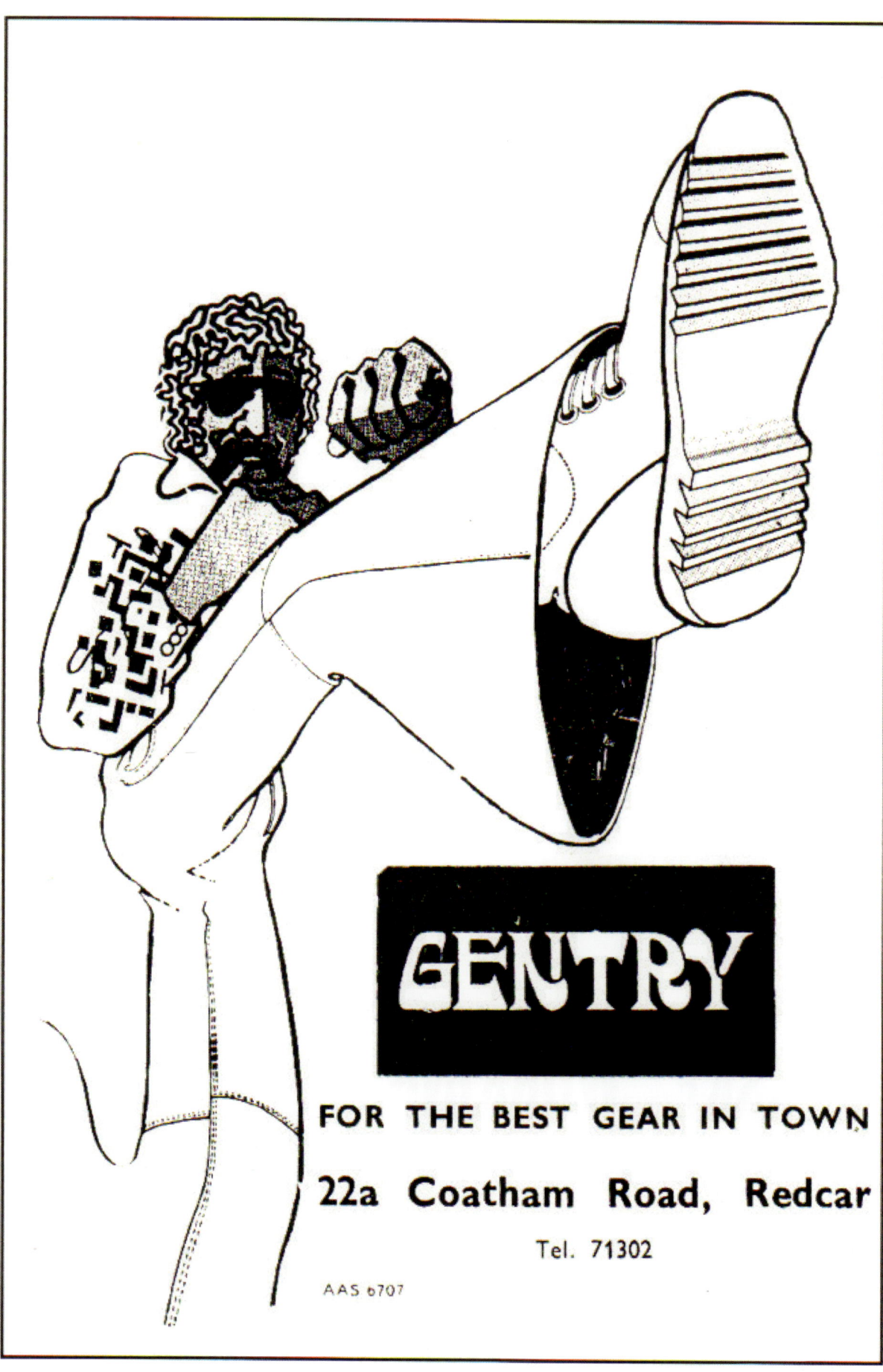

Deep Purple

By 1973 David had put together a band called The Fabulosa Brothers and gigged weekly in the locale. When it was announced in the music press that Ian Gillan was leaving Deep Purple and that they were welcoming tapes from unknown singers David saw a potential opportunity although he surely must have considered the likelihood extremely slim.

Once again Roger Barker helped out. "I rang up this company in London and said would they be interested in me sending them a tape of a singer." The tape in question was a rough recording by The Fabulosa Brothers but Deep Purple was suitably impressed to give him a try.

As David recalled, "The demo featured my local band, 'The Fabulosa Brothers'… a bunch of great blokes, and great players. We had recently made some demos of Harry Nilsson's 'Everybody's Talking', done as a boogie. Bill Wither's 'Lonely Town, Lonely Street' and probably 'Ain't No Sunshine'. We would take these songs and rearrange them to suit our funk/rock approach. The problem was after getting minimal support from the house engineer at 10cc's Strawberry Sound Studios in Stockport I had taken to drinking. Actually, rather a lot of drinking so my diction was somewhat 'slurred', to say the least. Ian Paice told me later it was my 'tone' that attracted him and Ritchie. They could hear I was well oiled."

"They heard the tape and rang again and said, 'Can you bring him down for an audition?' This was at forty-eight hours notice," recalls Barker. "Scorpio Studios in London. In came Deep Purple. He auditioned. Didn't know any of their stuff as such. I always remember he sang an incredible sort of heavy — 'cos he put the act on — version of 'Yesterday' by The Beatles. They snapped him up!"

David recalled it thus: "I told them I'd learned 'Strange Kind Of Woman' and we proceeded to 'blues' it up. Ritchie looked at me and said the way I was interpreting the song was how he'd envisaged it sounding when he wrote it. Then he says 'okay you can sing rock, let's see what you can do with a ballad. Do you know the Beatles song 'Yesterday'? I think that one actually got me the gig."

Having spent the previous few years in semi-professional bands the start of a phenomenal career had begun.

For Deep Purple it had only taken a couple of months to complete the new line-up after which the immediate requirement was to record new material for a new album. After rehearsing at Clearwell Castle in the Forest of Dean, the *Burn* album was recorded in Montreux in November.

With the album completed the new look Deep Purple played five European shows in Denmark, Sweden, Belgium, Germany and Austria in December.

"It was 9th December 1973, when I had the indescribable honour of walking onstage with the extraordinary talents of Ritchie Blackmore, Jon Lord, Ian Paice & Glenn Hughes at the KB Halle in Copenhagen, Denmark for the very first time. The Burn album had yet to be released, but it showed the balls of the guys in the band to go out & play brand new, unheard songs to a rapturous Danish audience. An unforgettable experience for me."

Initially David and Glenn would find themselves in the awkward situation of receiving presentation discs for sales of albums by the previous line-ups as can be seen here where the band was awarded gold discs in Brussels whilst in town for the gig at the Forest-Vorst Nationa(a)l.

As David mentioned, with the album unreleased the show consisted almost entirely of new songs the public were unfamiliar with. The set list for these shows was:

Burn
Might Just Take Your Life
Lay Down, Stay Down
Mistreated
Smoke On The Water
Your Fool No One
Space Truckin'
What's Goin' On Here

1974

An extraordinary year in David Coverdale's life as the popularity of Purple grew beyond his wildest dreams.

Stadthalle, Bremen, 18th September 1974
© Roland Güder

PURPLE HIT Coventry with two evenings of good music and sheer lunacy to mark the end of a triumphant British tour. Everything seemed quite normal at the opening of Elf's set. They have developed into a highly polished professional unit. Ronnie Dio displayed his powerful vocals on a searing rendition of "Happy" from their current album "Carolina County Ball" and the delivery of this number was so crisp and powerful that the audience surged towards the stage in appreciation.

Suddenly from nowhere a "dirty great big" bag of flour hit Ronnie on the head. More of them seemed to appear from the corners of the stage and soon enough the whole line-up of Stephen Edwards (guitar), Craig Gruber (bass), Mickey Lee Soule (piano) and Cool Guy (drums) were covered in dat white stuff. The audience, who were looking a bit dead, didn't seem to react to this attack.

Next on were Purple, kicking the set off in fine form with "Burn". They played their asses off and the set ran smoothly apart from a mysterious incident involving a bottle breaking against the side of Glenn Hughes leg. Blackmore featured some really fine soloing and Ian Paice did a mindblasting solo in "You Fool No One" which went into "Mule". David Coverdale displayed his vociferous vocals in "Mistreated". It was a great set, not their best, but they were out to have a good time.

They too were bombarded with flour at the end of "Space Trucking". By this time the audience were on their feet and cheering and the band came back on for an encore which was "Going Down" which culminated with a line of trouserless roadies having a knees up across the stage. To finish this off a certain gentleman, who has been described as the entertainments officer, strode across the stage in black tights, knee-length boots and hat, looking like the son of Max Wall, and bared his buttocks to all.

Backstage after the show the scene was comparitively calm. Jon, Dave and Glenn were getting ready for their trip to Germany the next day where they will be performing Jon's "Gemini Suite" and everyone was bidding each other farewell. Two burly characters confronted me. "don't forget to mention Pad of the plank and Jim for their excellent job on security", uh okay, boys.

Birmingham Odeon, 4th May 1974
© Laurens van Houten / Frank White Photo Agency

Birmingham Odeon, 4th May 1974
© Laurens van Houten / Frank White Photo

Stadthalle, Bremen, 18th September 1974
© Roland Güder

In action with Deep Purple in Hamburg, 30th March 1975
© Roland Güder

1975

Although Glenn Hughes had been earmarked to join Purple for several months and took on his role ahead of David, the two bonded together well and continue a close relationship to this day.

Ernst-Merck-Halle, Hamburg, 30th March 1975
© Roland Güder

DEEP PURPLE: "Come Taste The Band" (Purple Records) Jon Lord (keyboards); Ian Paice (drums); Tommy Bolin (guitar); David Coverdale (bass); Glenn Hughes (vocals). Produced by Deep Purple and Martin Birch. Recorded at Munich's Musicland Studios.

DEEP Purple, as a band, have suffered from a mass musical malaise for some time now. Their last album "Stormbringer" typified this to a startling exent. As Jon Lord agrees, the band had become tired and bored and it showed.

"Stormbringer" was certainly not what Deep Purple were about. Instead of a heads-up onslaught on the senses, relieved on occasion with more melodic classically-influenced breaks, the album was so laidback it was almost horizontal. Now, of course, Ritchie Blackmore has left the band and his replacement Tommy Bolin shows what a difference can be wrought in an apparently dormant band by the addition of just one new member.

In total, "Come Taste The Band" comes across as an album made by a fresh, alive and creative unit — light years from the tedium of "Stormbringer." It is not easy to overstate the influence of Bolin. For a start, he wrote eight of the tracks on this ten track opus and he's obviously had a great deal of freedom given him by the other five in shaping the band's musical direction. Furthermore, he is an inventive and tasteful guitarist — Blackmore is able enough, to be sure, but in the context of Purple he had become just a trifle stereotyped. Bolin, on the other hand, is shiny, new and untainted by Purple's long-standing musical and personal problems.

The album starts in fine roaring style with "Comin' Home," a metal-sharp belter which gives Hughes plenty of room for his vocal pyrotechnics. "Lady Luck," "Gettin' Tighter" and "Dealer" continue the theme of power, with just a hint of malevolence showing through on the latter through Coverdale's moody bass lines. "Owed To G," despite it's irritating and ersatz underground title, and "Love Child" give Lord a chance to shine. And it must be stated here that the man is a pretty fine keyboardist. He tends at times to overstate the classicism in his style but, one feels, his solo excursions are going a long way to expunge the more obvious and hence annoying traits in this formalised approach.

A good album, representative of Purple and a promising indicator of things to come. They may never achieve again the public and critical acceptance which was theirs with past efforts but they show here that they're still a viable band, capable of producing exciting and interesting music. — B.H.

O Lord, why hast thou forsaken us?

DEEP PURPLE: Come Taste The Band (Purple)

THERE ARE two points to make about this album straightaway. One is that new guitarist Tommy Bolin proves to be a considerable source of material and inspiration and has laid down as many solos in one set as other guitarists would in four.

And secondly that Jon Lord, one of the two remaining originals, is out to lunch throughout most of the set. Which could of course be indicative of disinterest . . . or because Bolin has the stronger musical personality and is as smart as Ritchie Blackmore when it comes to grabbing the spotlight.

For this, and more, the album is a real curiosity. It's probably their best since, let's say, "In Rock", epitomising perfectly all the name Deep Purple represented: high energy, barrel-rolling power and uncomprising rock and roll at its very best. But it's basically the new boys who've produced this.

Ian Paice rows himself in once on a joint composition with Bolin and David Coverdale, and Lord teams up with Glenn Hughes for a beautifully mellow track called "This Time Around", which makes Jon's trip out to Munich's Musicland Studios worthwhile after all, while the rest of the album is taken care of by (predominantly) Coverdale and Bolin, with Hughes snatching another two joint composing honours with one or the other.

So you've got to agree that it's a pretty strange situation for three rookies to know more about the concept of Deep Purple than a coupla founding members obviously do.

Paice, however, does show he's an invaluable member when it actually comes to laying down the rhythms on that kit, and he and Hughes have the kind of professional relationship (at least on record) which can only be described as Hot Shit. There is after all more power and time changing, accent-making ingenuity than ever before in a Purple line-up.

Naturally it then follows that Bolin should play a dual role. One, as "Gettin' Tighter" illustrates, to brace thick, energy-packed chords into the rhythm, and two, as a lead soloist of such tremendous talent that despite the excellent vocal harmonies of Coverdale and Hughes on the soulful "I Need Love," he again steals the glory for his outstanding work.

This man is an absolute maniac. Not only can he bleed the licks out on an overdrive piece such as "Comin' Home", but he can restrict what seems a naturally extrovert style (requiring quite frequently double tracking to do what he must do but whichisn't humanly possible with only one outlet) to become almost conservative. When required — as in the dramatic tension of "Drifter", where Bolin unloops the melody line to allow Hughes and Paice to battle their way through.

And Lord dozes off in the corner.

Well he has one other moment, besides the one mentioned earlier. And that's during "You Keep On Movin'", where Bolin effectively cuts a path for the organ to surface and then frames the resulting solo.

Maybe Lord felt he couldn't contribute much more, even though that one solo is truly worthwhile and something similar elsewhere would have been a welcome contrast. Yet there's also Coverdale straining for vocal space, and justly getting it, so Lord's obviously observing the old Too Many Cooks proverb.

Whatever, Deep Purple are alive and well. This album proves it.

Tony Stewart

Across the water the sun is shining

David's time with Deep Purple came to an inglorious end after a brief UK tour in 1976. For founding members Jon Lord and Ian Paice, they had come to the end of the road. For David, having only experienced the high life for two and a half years, he suddenly found himself at a loose end. During the summer he was approached by Uriah Heep who were looking for a replacement for departed vocalist David Byron. Bassist John Wetton had also left Heep. Former Bedlam bassist Denny Ball was auditioned as Wetton's replacement. In an interview Ball recalled, "The line up almost became: Denny Ball / Mick Box / David Coverdale / Ken Hensley / Lee Kerslake. I have good memories of the rehearsal when Dave Coverdale sang with us. I don't think Coverdale wanted the gig in the end, but it was out of my hands, and I was very, very disappointed not to join the band. The rehearsal with Coverdale was recorded off the mixing console by the road crew at the time. These were just cassettes, and I don't know what would have happened to them. They were probably used at the assessment meeting, which decided the eventual line up of the band. As for what we played at the session, most of it was jamming, with a couple of Chuck Berry songs thrown in for good measure. I can remember Lee Kerslake particularly enjoyed himself."

When Coverdale was interviewed for *Let it Rock*, in 2008 he commented, "Actually, it was not really an audition, I never had any intention of going there. I just jammed with Heep for fun. Nice guys, but it was never a career consideration. I knew what I wanted to do – and I did it. It was too similar musically to what Purple were doing, and I definitely preferred Purple. I really did know what I wanted to do."

"There were three things I was offered after Purple. Tony Iommi, God bless his cotton socks, was calling me a lot, and I was saying: 'Tony, I love you but I know what I want to do'. I think Sabbath are amazing at what they do but it wasn't something that I wanted to do. The most interesting one is mostly unknown. There was a management guy who got in touch with me and asked if I'd be interested in singing with Jeff Beck, Willie Weeks, Andy Newmark and Jean Rousseau. Rousseau was the keyboard player with Cat Stevens. I would have dropped pretty much everything for that. This was right before Whitesnake in 1976 or early '77."

In August whilst living in Munich David started work on his first solo album with the help of Micky Moody, his longstanding friend from Middlesbrough and Roger Glover who produced it. *White Snake* was launched the following year in the middle of a music scene dominated by Punk and Disco and received very little accolade.

Unperturbed David's second album, *Northwinds* continued his development as a songwriter with Glover once again in the producer's chair and Micky Moody, providing the musical backbone as well as contributing to the songwriting.

> *"Micky and I enjoyed working together and got on well enough as friends at that time. He was a local musical hero of mine. I thought he had great potential. He was aware and supportive of my desire for a hard rock, blues-based, melodic rock band... with soul! He was also the antithesis of Ritchie Blackmore.*

The release of *Northwinds* also saw David go back on the road to promote it. With Moody they put together a band to play a few tiny clubs in England. Bernie Marsden came in from the recently defunct Paice Ashton Lord along with Neil Murray formerly of Colosseum II on bass, and from Roger Chapman's band Streetwalkers came drummer David Dowle and keyboard player Brian Johnstone.

The very first show was at Lincoln College of Technology on 3rd March 1978. Whilst the band was billed as David Coverdale's Whitesnake some gig adverts simply billed them under David's name only.

During these early shows the band also included a few Deep Purple songs such as 'Lady Luck', Lady Double Dealer' and 'Mistreated'.

Coverdale tour

DAVID COVERDALE, former lead vocalist with Deep Purple, goes on a major UK tour in March with his band. The band line-up is Micky Moody guitar, Bernie Marsden guitar, David Dowell (ex-Streetwalkers) drums and Neil Murray (ex-Colosseum) bass.

The tour coincides with the release of Coverdale's second solo album, 'Northwinds', from which is taken his new single, 'Breakdown'.

Full dates for the tour are: Lincoln Technical College March 3, Folkestone Leescliff Hall 4, Wolverhampton Lafayette 5, Ilford Oscars 8, Scarborough Penthouse 9, Harrogate PJs 10, Basingstoke Technical College 17, London Music Machine 18, Newbridge Club 19, Manchester Rafters 21, Doncaster Outlook 23, Redcar Coatham Bowl 24, Leeds Fforde Green Hotel 25, Colwyn Bay Pier 27, Plymouth Castaways 29, Swansea Nutz 30, Newport (Shropshire) Village 31.

DAVE COVERDALE

> *"Whitesnake were actually formed to promote Northwinds on a one-off promotional tour. I didn't know whether it would survive. There weren't many people backing this unfashionable horse."*

A week after the tour Whitesnake (now with Pete Solley on keyboards) went into the studios to cut their first recordings and released in May as the *Snakebite* EP. Whitesnake was up and running.

"Micky and I were both avid Allman Brothers fans. Lynyrd Skynyrd as well. Anything with that kind of bluesy guitar. There weren't many people in Britain doing it. But David loved that kind of feeling. I'd throw in some Albert King and Micky would do his bit, and suddenly it all started coming together. We went up to David's house in Archway, North London and wrote 'Come On' more or less straight away. I thought how great it was to be writing for a guy with such a great blues voice." Bernie Marsden

The third ever Whitesnake gig at Club Lafayette, Wolverhampton, 5th March 1978. "There were about 100 in the audience that included Ian Paice," remembers photographer Alan Perry.

More photos from this show follow on pages 27-31. All © Alan Perry.

> *"Believe it or not, it wasn't really my intention for the early Whitesnake to follow that blues kind of direction. It just began to develop as we played more and more together. Remember also at the beginning we had to do some Purple tunes to fill out the set."*

March 4th, 1978

Coverdale's band on debut outing

THE DEBUT British tour by ex-Deep Purple vocalist David Coverdale and his new band, plans for which were exclusively revealed by NME in January, has now been confirmed. As reported, the line-up comprises ex-Streetwalkers drummer David Dowell, ex-Colosseum bassist Neil Murray and guitarists Micky Moody and Bernie Marsden, and it's understood they be known as White Snake.

The tour ties in with the release of Coverdale's second EMI solo album "Northwinds", from which the single "Breakdown" has just been issued.

Dates are Lincoln Technical College (tomorrow, Friday), Folkestone Leas Cliff Hall (Saturday), Wolverhampton Lafayette (Sunday), Ilford Oscar's (March 8), Scarborough Penthouse (9), Harrogate P.G.'s Club (10), Basingstoke Technical College (17), London Camden Music Machine (18), Newbridge Club & Institute (19), Manchester Rafters (21), Doncaster Outlook (23), Redcar Coatham Bowl (24), Leeds Fforde Green Hotel (25), Colwyn Bay Dixieland Show-bar (27), Plymouth Castaways (29), Swansea Nutz Club (30) and Newport Village Club (31).

> *"Whitesnake's music had such a great feeling to it. The band were all highly rated musicians and it showed in the performances. Of course, we were into the blues – people like the Paul Butterfield Blues Band; we listened to that kind of stuff. We were all heavily influenced by John Mayall's Bluesbreakers and their 'Beano' album. I did like The Yardbirds with Jimmy Page; that almost psychedelic tinge they had. It was exciting."*
> Micky Moody

By the summer Jon Lord had joined. Just in time to help Whitesnake complete the debut album *Trouble.* In October the first bout of serious touring began, concluding at London's Hammersmith Odeon on 23rd November. The show was recorded for the Japanese record company and released in March '79.

Although some of the Deep Purple songs had been dropped, with Lord now in the band, 'Might Just Take Your Life' was brought into the set. "It's an excellent feature for Jon and once again we re-arranged it to suit the band Whitesnake," said David at the time.

> *"David talked me into joining. He was calling me for six months and then in August of '78, I finally said yes."*
> Jon Lord

DAVID COVERDALE, PETE SOLLEY (SPECIAL GUEST), BERNIE MARSDEN, DAVE DOWLE, NEIL MURRAY, MICKY MOODY.
DAVID COVERDALE'S WHITESNAKE

At the Intercontinental in Cologne, 13th December 1978
© Marc Brans

At the Intercontinental in Cologne, 13th December 1978
Above: with Jon Lord and below: with Lord and Whitesnake crew member Ossie Hoppe.

Birmingham Odeon, 2nd November 1978
© Alan Perry

Birmingham Odeon, 2nd November 1978
© Alan Perry

"What people don't necessarily realise is that myself, David, Micky and Bernie all came out of the formative period of 1966 to 1967, when the blues was really the booming thing in Britain. When I started playing professionally in 1974 I took it more into the jazz-fusion area. But when the opportunity came to join Whitesnake, it just brought out what was latent in my past." Neil Murray

In May '79 the band travelled to Clearwell Castle in Gloucestershire. David had been introduced to the press there six years earlier when he had joined Deep Purple. Now in control of his own band they recorded the second album and the following month toured Germany.

When it was announced soon after that Ian Paice was to replace David Dowle, the press had a field day, claiming that there was a master plan to reform Deep Purple. With the new line-up Whitesnake headlined the Reading Festival in August and finished the year with a nineteen-date British tour, promoting the new album.

Reading Festival, 26th August 1979
© Alan Perry

"Paicey and Lordy coming in was the icing on the cake. They nailed the foundations and we took it from there. But the pressure of coming up with two albums' worth of original material every year proved too much for me as a singer and as a writer. For all of us, it just got too much. But we certainly jammed a lot of good stuff in those initial three or four years."

Reading Festival, 26th August 1979
© Alan Perry

Liverpool Empire, 4th November 1979
© Alan Perry

Liverpool Empire, 4th November 1979
© Alan Perry

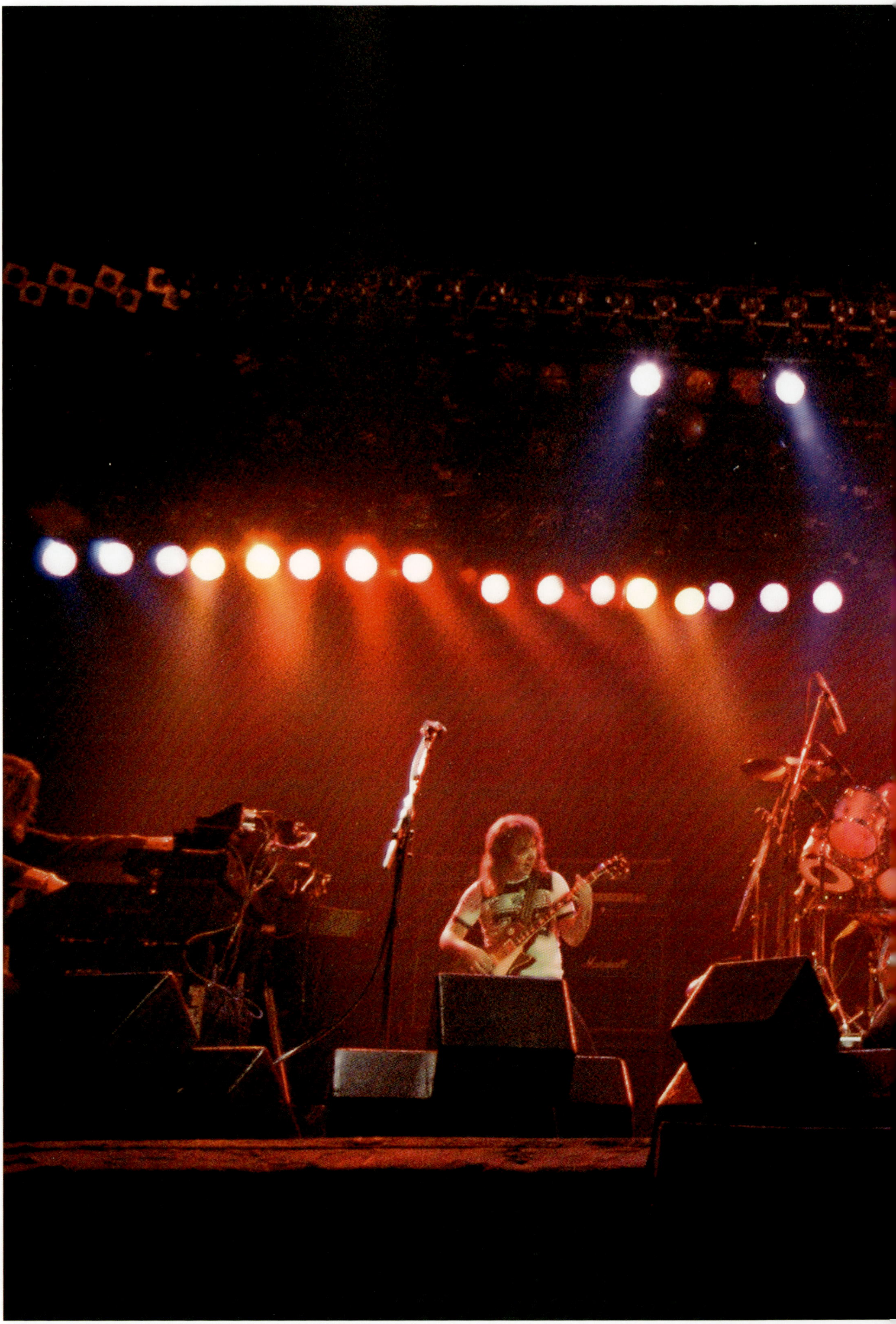

"It was great. We went on the road with a Mercedes van, with the gear in the back and seats for all of us, in the front and in the middle. Me, David and Micky would usually sit together in the middle row. It was a little family on the road with this huge star of Deep Purple. But David was just an ordinary bloke to me."
Bernie Marsden

Liverpool Empire, 4th November 1979.
© Alan Perry

Madison Square Garden, New York, USA, 9th October 1980.

© Bill O'Leary

The Eighties

The eighties started on a high for Whitesnake. The band's third album *Ready An' Willing* (released in May 1980), and the first with Ian Paice on drums, was also their first top ten album in the UK. The single taken from it, 'Fool For Your Loving' also made the top twenty. The following month a full-length UK tour ensued. October saw the first lengthy US tour as support to Jethro Tull.

David was still in the early stages of building the Whitesnake name in America, and by the end of the decade his achievements exceeded expectations.

Madison Square Garden, New York, USA, 9th October 1980.

"The early days were without question totally necessary. Everything needs a beginning, a foundation in order to grow. I couldn't have asked for a better way to start the ball rolling, or better players and people to be involved with."

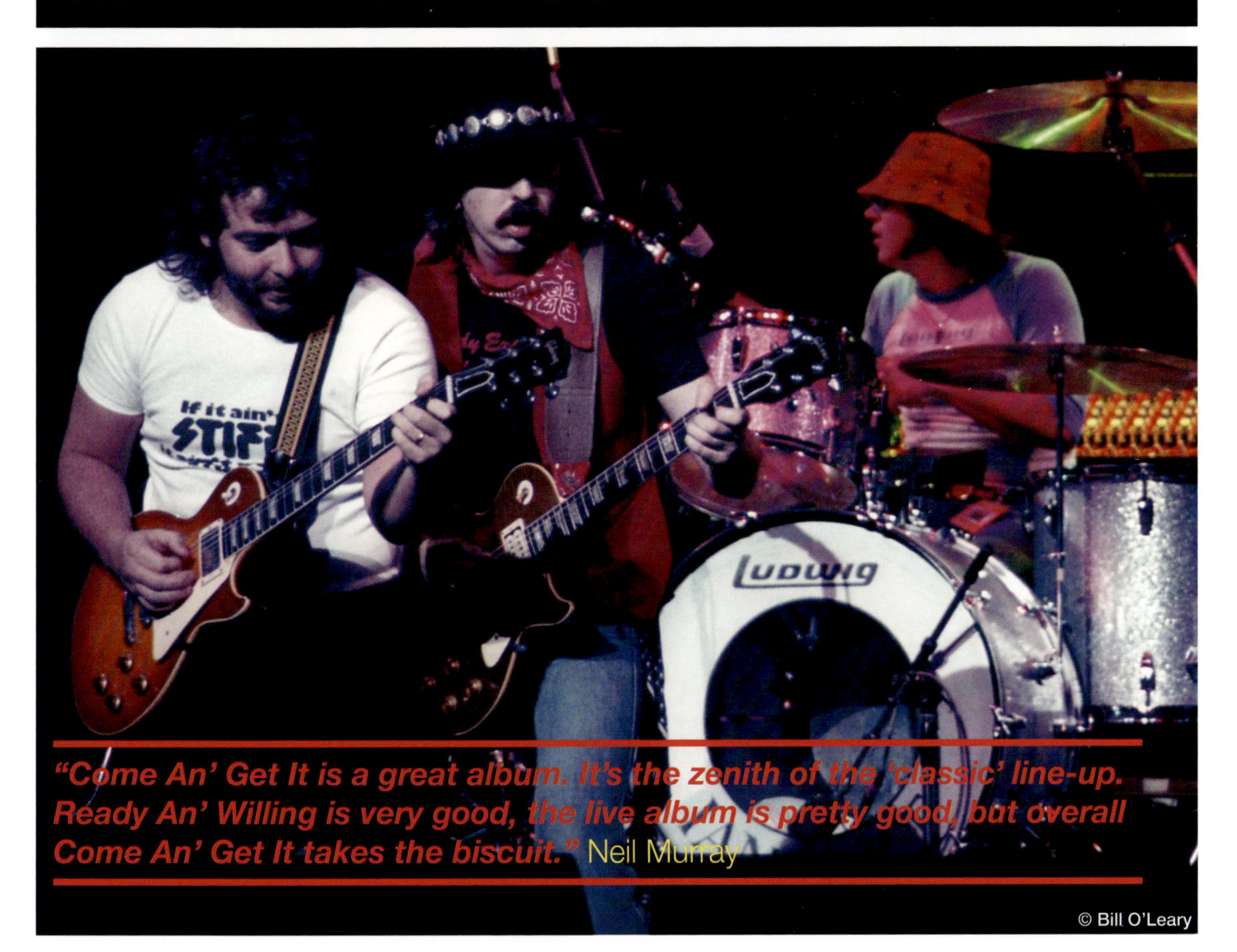

"Come An' Get It is my favourite of the early Whitesnake albums. It's down to the band's performance and the consistency of the songs. Production's good from Birchy too."

"Come An' Get It is a great album. It's the zenith of the 'classic' line-up. Ready An' Willing is very good, the live album is pretty good, but overall Come An' Get It takes the biscuit." Neil Murray

© Bill O'Leary

Inset: Germany, 1981
© Neil Murray

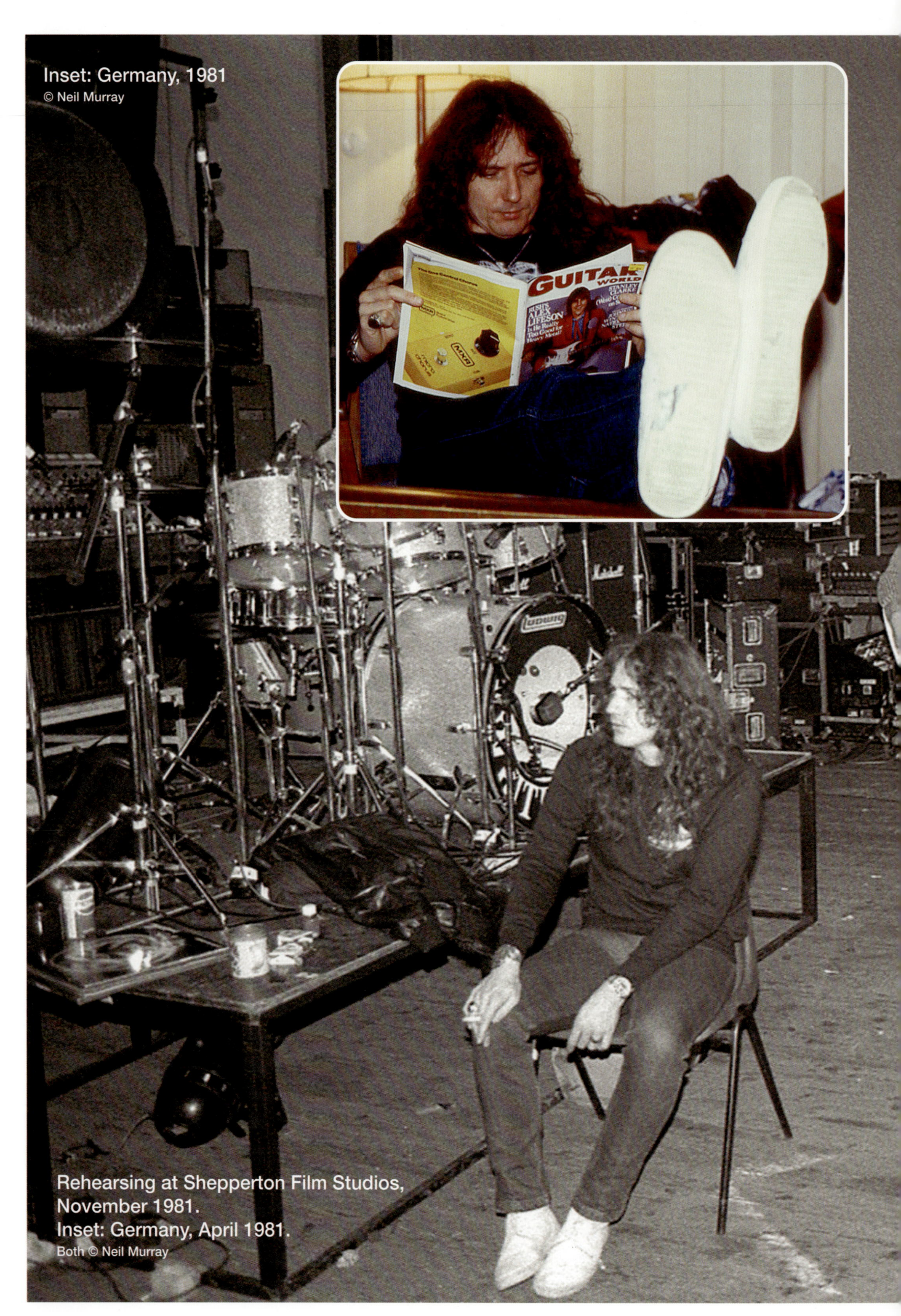

Rehearsing at Shepperton Film Studios, November 1981.
Inset: Germany, April 1981.
Both © Neil Murray

1981 saw the band's UK success continue to rise. *Come an' Get It* went straight into the album charts at number 2 and was only kept off the top spot by Adam & The Ants! The first single released from the album, 'Don't Break My Heart Again' was also another top twenty hit. Not bad for a group seen essentially as an album band.

Following the release of the album, pretty much the rest of the year saw the band touring mainland Europe, UK, Japan and USA as the Whitesnake juggernaut kicked into overdrive. A highlight of the year was the band's appearance at the second Monsters of Rock Festival at Donington Park, second on the bill to AC/DC.

1982's *Saints & Sinners* would prove to be the last from this line-up and when Whitesnake returned to the Monsters of Rock Festival in 1983 as headliners, the band consisted of Micky Moody and Jon Lord, along with Mel Galley (Guitar), Colin Hodgkinson (Bass) and Cozy Powell (Drums).

Forest National, Brussels, 28th January 1983.
All insets: Forest National, Brussels, 6th September 1983
© Marc Brans

Whitesnake in 1982.
Left to right:
Colin Hodgkinson,
Mel Galley, Cozy Powell,
Jon Lord, David Coverdale,
Micky Moody.
(AF archive / Alamy Stock Photo)

"I have a big 65" TV in my gym to try to distract me from the pain in my knees and it's wired into Apple TV so I can access all my photographs. I have around 20,000 photos on there. I put in on shuffle and there's lots of personal photos on there and lots of music related photos too. When a picture from the Slide It In era of Whitesnake came up half the band has passed away. Jon Lord, Mel Galley and Cozy Powell are all now gone and that's such a shame. It's chilling, it just stops you in your tracks. I really miss them all; they were great musicians and fantastic to play with. Loss is tough and to find the time to grieve and process that is difficult particularly in a public scenario."

Backstage at Forest National, Brussels, 28th January 1983.
© Marc Brans

"It may well have been that David wanted a complete change. At the end of the Saints & Sinners recordings, there came a time when he was splitting from not only the management, but also from the publishing and record companies. It was quite a major thing to do. He had to buy himself out. So he may well have said: 'Okay, I'm going to start completely afresh with a new band, we'll see what happens after that.' Who knows?"
Neil Murray

The first major transformation came with 1984's *Slide It In*. With a new record company in the States, following its UK release in January, Geffen insisted that it be revamped. With John Sykes being brought in for Moody and Neil Murray returning, the US release was vastly overhauled to give it a more contemporary sound. This was vindicated as it gave Whitesnake its first serious success in America, breaking into the top forty. Greater things were still to come...

But before they did Jon Lord departed for the Deep Purple reunion of the MKII line up and with Mel Galley sidelined Whitesnake was stripped back to a four piece as the band performed to one of the biggest audiences of their career at the massive Rock In Rio Festival in 1985.

The same year David and John Sykes started writing new material for the next planned album but all manner of things meant that despite being recorded and completed by April 1986 the album would not be released for another year.

This saw huge transformations to Whitesnake both sonically and visually. The self-titled album, often referred to as 1987 would become the zenith of Whitesnake's career. It was a massive success in the States, reaching number two on the Billboard chart. The album also spawned several hit singles. A re-recording of 'Here I Go Again' reached number one in the States and 'Is This Love' made number two.

After ten years and numerous ups and downs David could enjoy the fruits of his labour as Whitesnake became one of the biggest bands of the late eighties.

"I'd met David Geffen and John Kalodner and I was fascinated by them. I'd been surrounded by a mentality that if you make five pounds profit let's go to the pub. Whereas David Geffen said, 'If You can make five dollars profit, why not 50? If 50 why not 500? Why not 50,000, why not five million?' I embraced that philosophy and it applied well in my career perspective."

March, 1987 © Ross Marino / MediaPunch

"I was about three million dollars in debt when the 1987 album was released and within three months I was in credit. That's how big it was and how quick it happened."

At The Limelite in Chicago, Illinois. July 20, 1987

© Gene Ambo / MediaPunch

David has always had many female admirers which might explain the stiletto heels and hairbrush that he and Adrian Vandenberg consult on during the show at the Brendan Byrne Arena in East Rutherford, New Jersey on 13th August 1988

© Frank White Photo Agency

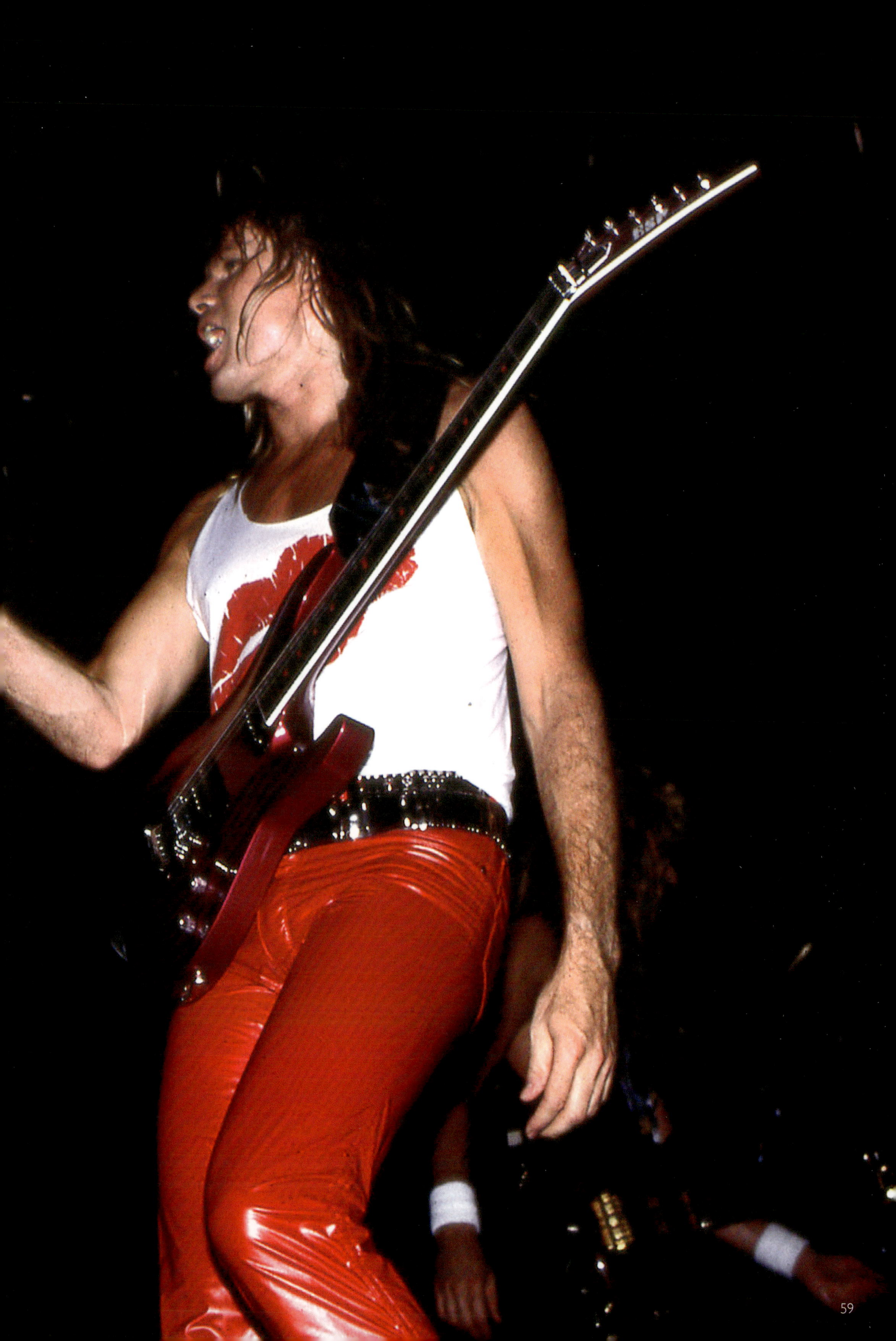

Brendan Byrne Arena,
East Rutherford,
New Jersey, 13th August 1988
© Frank White Photo Agency

Brendan Byrne Arena,
East Rutherford,
New Jersey, 13th August 1988
© Frank White Photo Agency

Peoria Civic Center, Illinois.
8th November 1987

© Gene Ambo / MediaPunch

Municipal Auditorium,
Nashville, Tennessee
8th March, 1988

© RTGwinn/MediaPunch

© Frank White Photo Agency

Orange County Speedway, Middletown, New York, 5th August 1988
© Frank White Photo Agency

Orange County Speedway,
Middletown, New York,
5th August 1988

© Frank White Photo Agency

Orange County Speedway, Middletown, New York, 5th August 1988

Munich, 24th November, 1989
© DPA Picture Alliance / Alamy Stock Photo

Munich, 24th November 1989 during promotion for *Slip Of The Tongue.*
© DPA Picture Alliance / Alamy Stock Photo

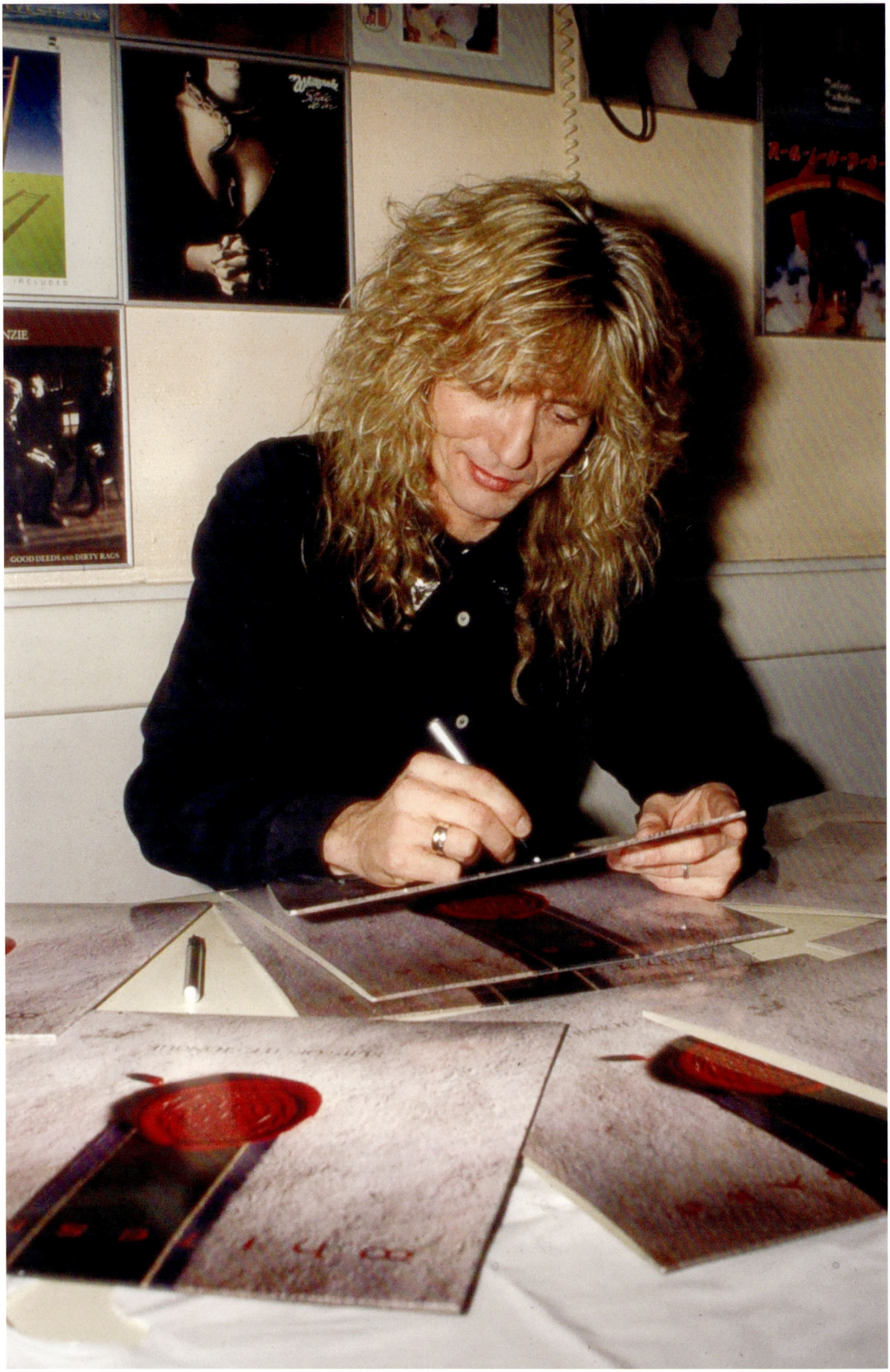
GOOD DEEDS AND DIRTY RAGS

More shots from Munich. Interestingly many of the albums pictured in the background were recorded at Musicland Studios in the city, including the two Deep Purple albums from David's own back catalogue as well as albums by his fellow Purple band members Blackmore, Lord and Paice.
© DPA Picture Alliance / Alamy Stock Photo

Brendan Byrne Arena, East Rutherford, New Jersey, 12th April 1990
© Frank White Photo Agency

90s

Following the huge success of the 1987 album was always going to be a tough call and although 1989's *Slip Of The Tongue* did well, the sales never matched those of its predecessor. Reflecting back on it David also had his reservations about the album.

"For a long time, I felt the album lacked a certain Whitesnake feel in the music, but, countless people through the years have assured me that they enjoyed and enjoy the album, nonetheless. So, now I happily accept it as a significant part of the Whitesnake catalogue and to be honest, I enjoy it more now than I did back then. It was an album plagued with challenges and obstacles for me, personally, from many avenues, but hey... nobody said being successful is supposed to be easy!"

But with Whitesnake firmly established within the landscape of American rock music the band toured on the strength of the album in 1990. It was the biggest undertaken by the band — five months playing huge arenas across the whole of the States.

After such a brilliant start to the evening from Bad English one also wondered how, or even if, David Coverdale and company could top it. For the thought to cross my mind I must have been mad, for not only did Whitesnake top it, they turned this into the most amazing gig I have ever been to. 'Supergroup' would be a label not good enough for this band.

Steve Price, Review taken from Metal Forces, Issue 50, 1990 of the show at The Summit, Houston, Texas, USA, March 16th, 1990.

A slip of the tongue for the ladies.

Brendan Byrne Arena, East Rutherford, New Jersey, 12th April 1990
© Frank White Photo Agency

David and Steve Vai in full flight.

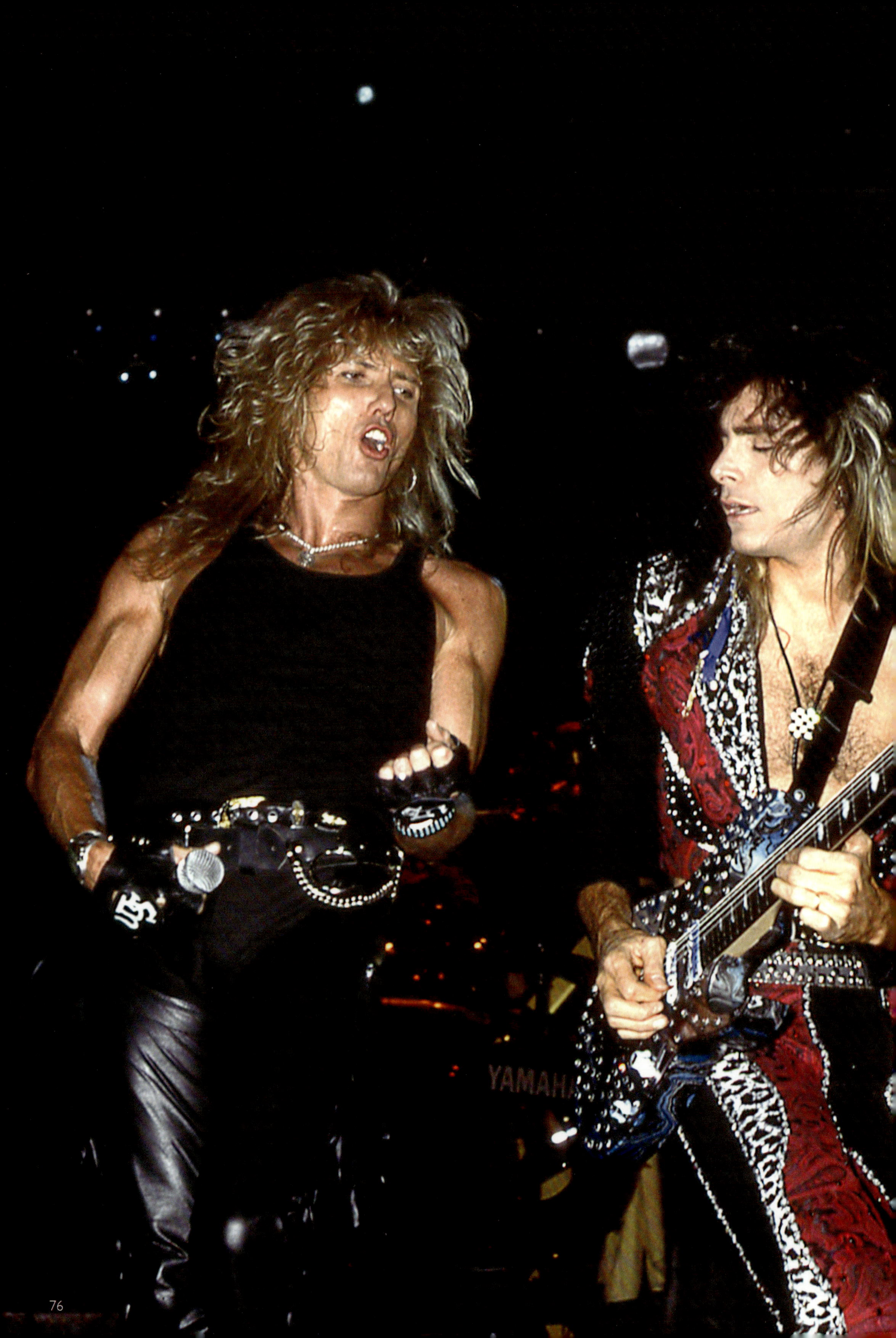
YAMAHA

"When Whitesnake came along — I mean, I liked the music of Whitesnake. That record that they released with 'Still Of The Night' and all that — that was huge. It sounded great, and David Coverdale's an incredible singer."

Steve Vai, Sleaze Roxx,
11th December 2016

Brendan Byrne Arena, East Rutherford, New Jersey, 12th April 1990
© Frank White Photo Agency

1990 also saw David involved with the film *Days Of Thunder*, contributing to the soundtrack with his performance of the Billy Idol / Hans Zimmer composition 'The Last Note Of Freedom'. It was also released as a single, a unique side step from the flamboyancy and grandiose of Whitesnake at its commercial peak.

"I was in the middle of the *Slip of the Tongue* tour and I was actually under the weather and normally I would have said no I don't have any time, but the huge carrot that attracted this old donkey was working with Trevor Horn. One of the greatest producers I've ever heard and it was an opportunity to work with him. I'd just finished a show in San Francisco so I took the opportunity of slipping home up to Tahoe, then chartered a plane, flew down, walked into the studio and said Trevor I'm as sick as a dog, if it doesn't work at least I've had the pleasure of working with you. He offered me a huge spliff, that was the medicine I needed."

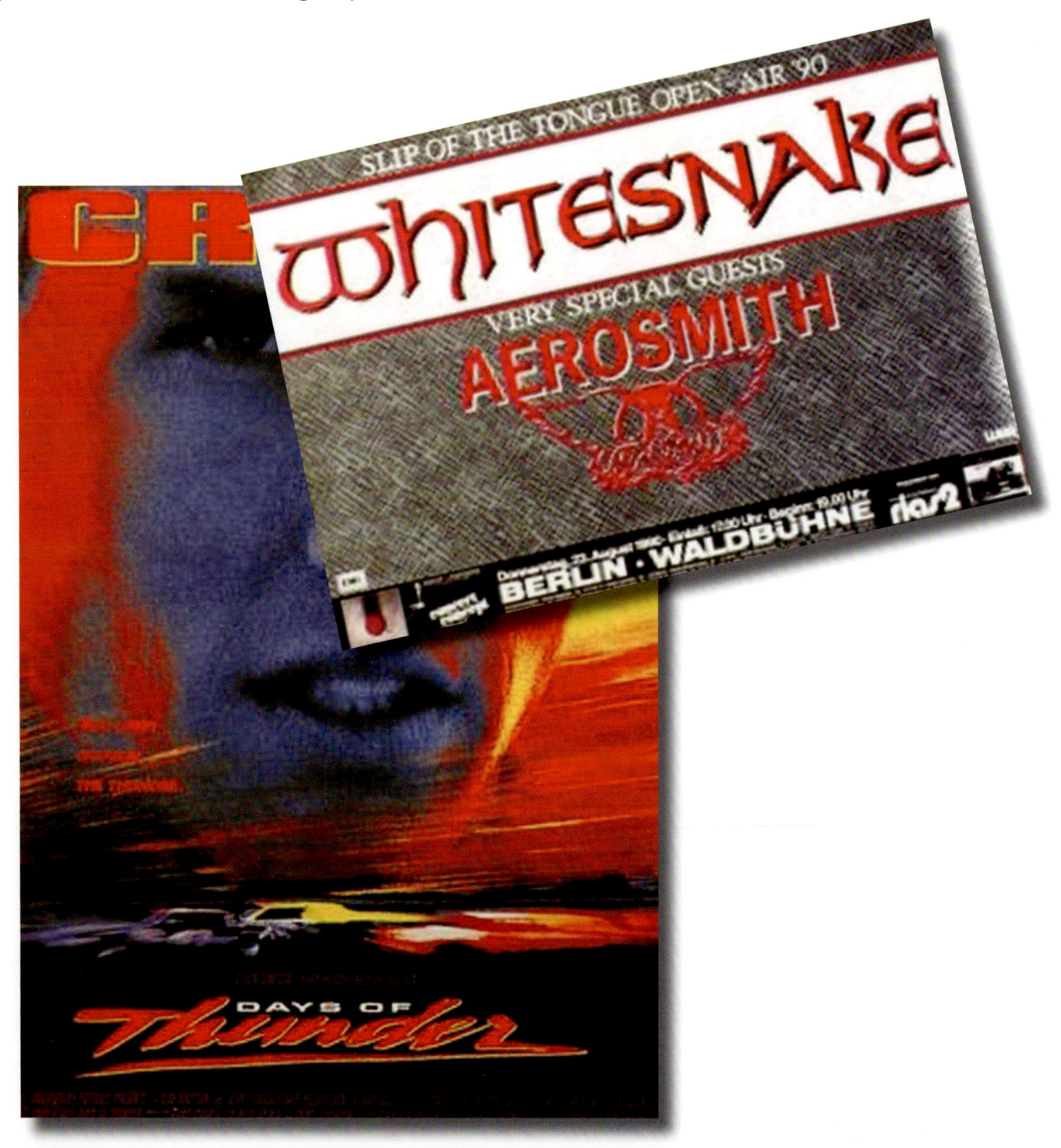

By August the Whitesnake juggernaut rolled into Europe with a mixture of arenas and outdoor gigs including the Monsters of Rock at Donington; the only UK show of the tour. It was Whitesnake's third appearance at the festival, and the second as the headlining act.

© DPA Picture Alliance / Alamy Stock Photo

Ready to go on stage at Donington. Left to right: Adrian Vandenberg, Steve Vai, David Coverdale, Tommy Aldridge & Rudy Sarzo.

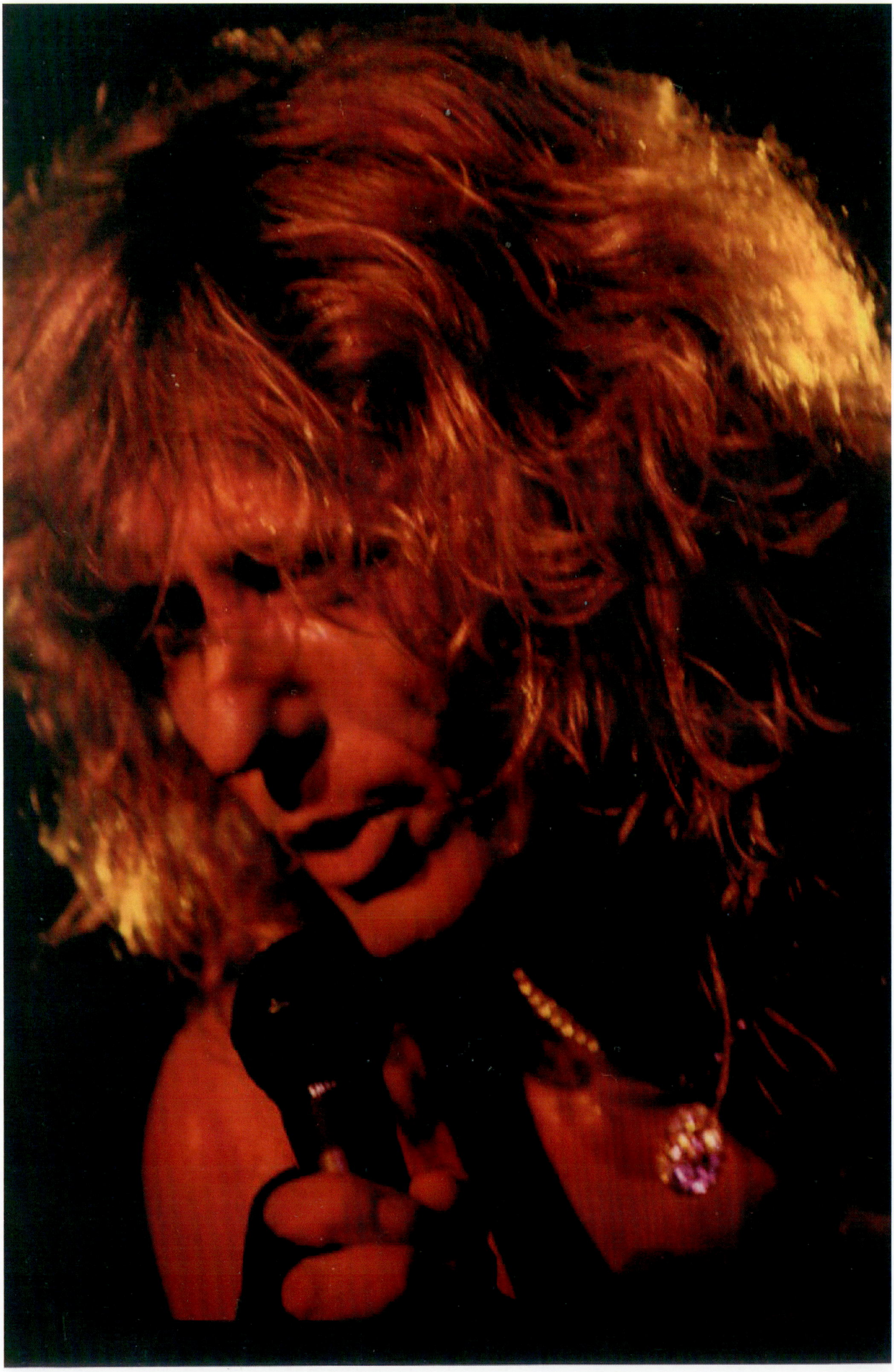

One of the last European shows of the Slip Of The Tongue tour at the Flanders Expo, Ghent, Belgium, 4th September 1990.
© Marc Brans

Tommy Aldridge, Rudy Sarzo, Steve Vai, David Coverdale & Adrian

MONSTERS OF ROCK 00262
04/09/90
GUEST
FLANDERS EXPO - GENT
Dinsdag 4 september 90 - 19 u.
Mardi 4 septembre 90 - 19 h.
MAKE IT HAPPEN present
MONSTERS OF ROCK
WHITESNAKE with
POISON — QUIREBOYS
GUEST 00262
DE PARKING OP FLANDERS EXPO IS BETALEND.
U kan uw parkingjeton ter plaatse aan de kassa
kopen voor 50 Fr.
LE PARKING DE FLANDERS EXPO EST PAYANT.
Vous pouvez acheter votre jeton à la caisse pour 50 Fr.
VERBODEN IN DE ZAAL : GLAZEN FLESSEN,
BLIKJES, BANDOPNEMERS EN FILM/FOTO CAMERA'S.
SONT INTERDITS DANS LA SALLE : BOUTEILLES EN
VERRE, CANETTES, ENREGISTREURS, CAMERAS ET
APPAREILS PHOTO.

David relaxing backstage at the Flanders Expo.
© Marc Brans

87

And enjoying a moment of frivolity with Steve Vai.

Alas the frivolity was coming to an end for the time being, following the last show of an exhausting tour at the famous Budokan in Tokyo on 26th September. "I gave all my stage clothes to Cathy, my wardrobe assistant, and said: "Burn 'em, get rid of 'em, I'm done." The band had no idea I'd filed for divorce from Tawny. In my mind it was my farewell performance. I hadn't stopped working for three or four years. Non-stop. And at the end of that last Tokyo show, I got all the guys together said: "Look, I've filed for divorce, I've gotta take a break and see if I still want to do this." I told them if they got an opportunity to go elsewhere, please take it. Please don't be calling me saying: "Are we gonna do anything?" Because I won't take the call. And I hugged 'em all and thanked 'em for a great tour."

The following year David's career took an unexpected twist. After a meeting with Led Zeppelin's Jimmy Page. "I got a call from my booking agent Rod MacSween going: 'Do you mind if I give your number to Jimmy Page?' Which was just way too interesting for me to pass. It was only a few months after putting the 'Snake on hold. And I said: 'You know, Jimmy, I'm going through what I know is going be a knockdown, drag-out divorce. I don't want to be distracted. If you don't mind, let's put it on the back burner for a while. But yes, I'd love to meet with you'."

"When Jimmy and I sat down to write, I'd jammed like a motherfucker the day before he was flying into Tahoe, and we utilised every idea on my 'ideas cassette'. It was the best medicine. Put yourself to creative work. You know, work you enjoy, while you're sorting out the other shit."

Jimmy Page

COVERDALE · PAGE

"I took the creative side of working with Jimmy Page very seriously because I'd been a fan and an admirer of Jimmy Page since way before Zeppelin. Page is a lovely, lovely, lovely man to work and to socialise with."

Photo Credit: Norman Seeff

David Coverdale

GEFFEN

© 1993 The David Geffen Company / Permission to reproduce limited to editorial uses in newspapers and other regularly published periodicals and television news programming.

In March 1993 Coverdale Page was launched to the world. It sold well but was caught up in the era of Grunge, Nirvana, Pearl Jam and the like. Appetite for gigs was coming hard to come by. A planned US tour for the summer was scrapped and only a handful of shows in Japan were performed.

"I think mistakes were made on both sides, and it just didn't happen. We did half a dozen Japanese shows, which were just great fun. It was great to work with him, and I wouldn't change a thing. But close to three years we worked on that album and all for six shows. I really love to perform, I love creating songs with the intention of taking them live."

Coincidentally the Japanese tour dates started at Tokyo's Budokan, where David had done his "farewell" performance three years earlier. The set was a mixture of tracks from their collaboration along with Zeppelin and Whitesnake songs: *Absolution Blues, Slide It In, Rock and Roll, Over Now, Kashmir, Pride and Joy, Take a Look at Yourself, Take Me for a Little While, In My Time of Dying, Here I Go Again, White Summer, Black Mountain Side, Don't Leave Me This Way, Shake My Tree, Still of the Night, Black Dog, The Ocean, Feeling Hot.*

"The whole arrangement for the Coverdale/Page project was to go directly to the theatres, to the stage, and nothing, not even a whisper, came from Jimmy's manager when the album was released. It was one of the singularly most frustrating periods of my professional career."

"I worked with Pagey for three years as Coverdale Page so I thought it was entirely appropriate to start working as David Coverdale in '94."

"After three years and six shows, I wanted to form a kind of Mad Dogs And Englishmen kind of band with girl singers and stuff. I had a whole cassette of all these songs that I wanted to do, from The Allman Brothers, Little Feat, Muddy Waters, Hendrix. Just to go out and play, naïvely have fun and bring the fun too."

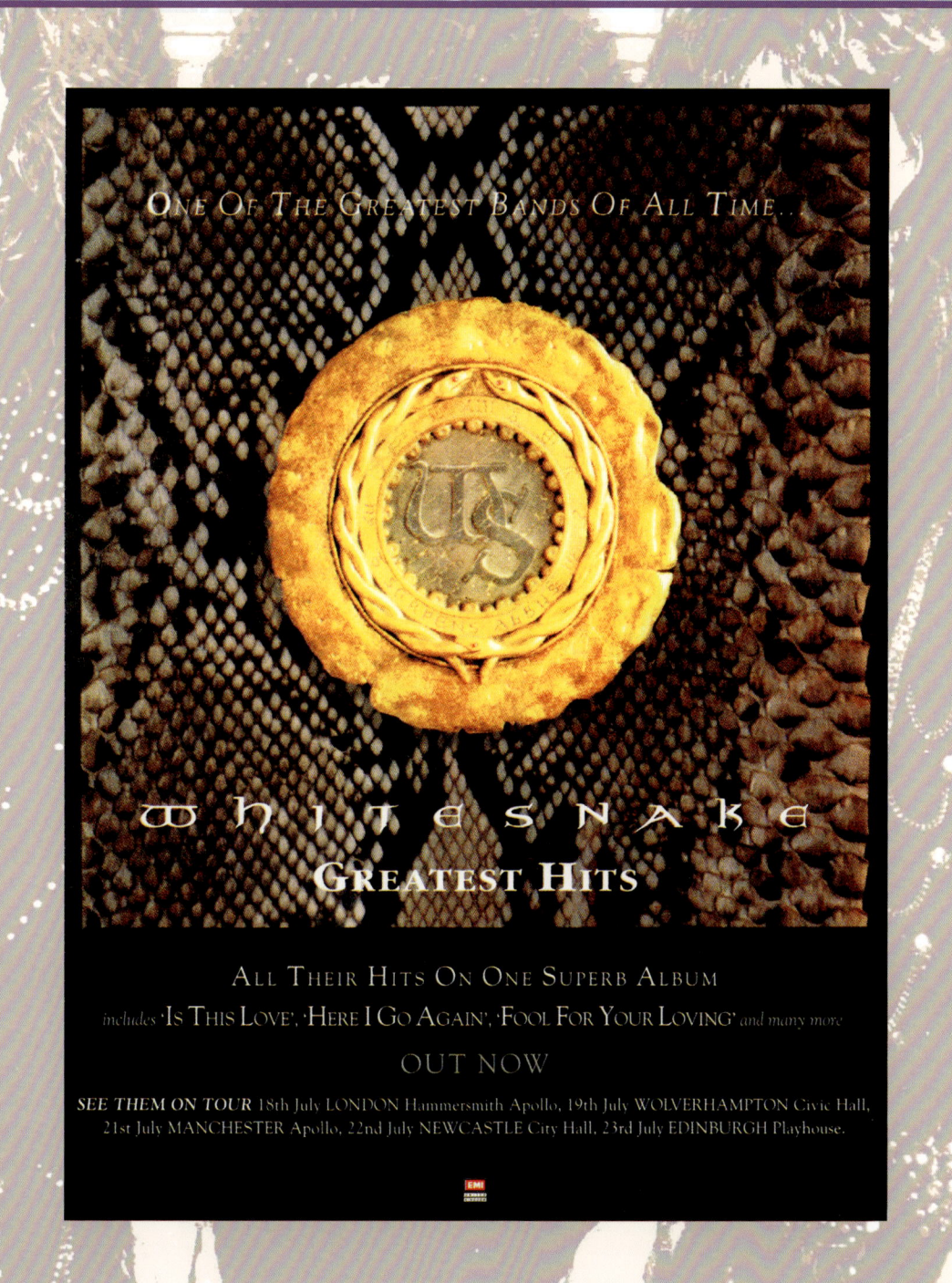

ONE OF THE GREATEST BANDS OF ALL TIME...

WHITESNAKE
GREATEST HITS

ALL THEIR HITS ON ONE SUPERB ALBUM
includes 'IS THIS LOVE', 'HERE I GO AGAIN', 'FOOL FOR YOUR LOVING' and many more
OUT NOW
SEE THEM ON TOUR 18th July LONDON Hammersmith Apollo, 19th July WOLVERHAMPTON Civic Hall, 21st July MANCHESTER Apollo, 22nd July NEWCASTLE City Hall, 23rd July EDINBURGH Playhouse.

> "I'm preparing this 'under the radar' European tour, and EMI decide to release Whitesnake's Greatest Hits, which went on to sell a million in the US. It also shifted a remarkable 100,000 records in two days in England, getting to number four in the chart! So I've got EMI on the phone to me, Rod MacSween on the phone to me, saying: "You gotta call it Whitesnake." I said: "I haven't formed a Whitesnake, this isn't what I would do as Whitesnake. So we went out and toured and the band were terrific, but I never considered it a Whitesnake thing, you know?"

Billed as the Whitesnake Greatest Hits Tour, it did good business in Europe, Japan and Australia, but missed out the States.

95

Viarock, Geraardsbergen, Belgium, 16th July 1994 © Marc Brans

Viarock, Geraardsbergen, Belgium, 16th July 1994 © Marc Brans

Viarock, Geraardsbergen, Belgium, 16th July 1994 © Marc Brans

To all intents and purposes Whitesnake was again put on hold as David focused on his first solo album since *Northwinds* in 1978.

"When it came to *Restless Heart,* the executives at EMI agreed with me after Coverdale Page that I could work as David Coverdale, they agreed I was gonna do a solo record. *Restless Heart* also started out as a solo record, and during the making of it, near the end, once again the guard at EMI changed and they said: 'We want this to be a Whitesnake record.' I was like: 'Fuck, it's not a Whitesnake record!' It was too late to start over, so we made the drums louder, we made the guitars louder. If you listen to that album and *Into The Light*, they're like brother and sister albums."

"The Restless Heart album was great. I really enjoyed the rock stuff. I enjoyed the whole album, actually. It was a difficult time for that type of music because so much was grunge at that point. I'm pretty convinced David will release it again sooner or later because it's a great album."
Adrian Vandenberg

Released in March 1997, *Restless Heart* once again saw David back on the road under the Whitesnake name. Prior to the tour, an acoustic show with Adrian Vandenberg was performed at EMI's studios in Japan and was released as *Starkers In Tokyo*, three days before the tour kicked off in Osaka.

Musikzirkus, Hanover, Germany, 17th October 1997

Musikzirkus, Hanover, Germany,
17th October 1997

Geisler-Fotopress GmbH / Alamy Stock Photo

Having accepted that *Restless Heart* be branded under the Whitesnake name, during press for the gigs David spoke of it being the farewell tour. Talking of the previous decade he said, "I just lost focus. And the goofiest thing was the more I lost focus, the more records I sold."

Slide It In went platinum and made the top 40, the enormously successful "1987" album was in the top 5 for more than six months, produced a bagful of hit singles and sold 10 million worldwide and *Slip Of The Tongue* also produced hit singles and went platinum.

"I thought what'd make you happy? What made you unhappy recently? Finishing Whitesnake with the overdecorated fucking Christmas tree that the *Slip Of The Tongue* record was. And I thought, you know what, I could finish it off properly, so I close the book with a smile."

Musikzirkus, Hanover, Germany,
17th October 1997

Geisler-Fotopress GmbH / Alamy Stock Photo

Into The New Millennium

> "I created the identity of Whitesnake and then I think ultimately became a victim of it."

David Coverdale entered the new millennium as a bona fide solo artist. He won his battle with EMI not to use the name Whitesnake for 2000's *Into The Light*. The album allowed him to stretch out, co-writing some of the songs with top session guitarist Earl Slick, who also performed on the album.

> "The new record is my ticket to the future and a salute to the past. It's still blues oriented but my voice isn't hidden behind a wall of guitars and thundering drums. So I don't know, maybe I've come full circle? But the record is called "Into The Light" and it is a lot more positive. This is a very positive period in my life. Everything seems to fall in its right place almost like by destiny. I'm convinced that things happen for a reason and I don't believe in coincidences anymore. I'll go where the inspiration takes me."

Although a success musically the album was more low key than his previous releases and by 2002 the temptation to reactivate Whitesnake was too much. With a new line-up of Tommy Aldridge on drums, Marco Mendoza (bass), Doug Aldrich (guitar), Reb Beach (guitar) and keyboard player Timothy Drury Whitesnake was back on the road in the States in late January 2003.

Back on the road as Whitesnake at Nassau Veterans' Memorial Coliseum, Uniondale, New York, 5th March 2003.
© Frank White Photo Agency

105

Extensive touring continued around the world right through to 2006 and was celebrated with a double live album *Live: In the Shadow of the Blues*. It also included four new studio songs but it wasn't until 2008 that a new Whitesnake album — *Good To Be Bad* was released — the first in almost a decade.

Graspop Metal, Dessel Belgium,
23rd June 2006
(Frank White Photo Agency)

In the intervening year, having moved to the States in the eighties, On 1st March 2007, David became a US citizen, in a ceremony in Reno, Nevada, and now holds dual US/UK citizenship.

Good To Be Bad Tour, Graspop Metal, Dessel Belgium, 27th June 2008
© Frank White Photo Agency

Good To Be Bad Tour, Graspop Metal, Dessel
Belgium, 27th June 2008
© Frank White Photo Agency

Good To Be Bad Tour, Graspop Metal, Dessel
Belgium, 27th June 2008
© Frank White Photo Agency

Arriving at the Classic Rock 'Roll Of Honour' at Park Lane Hotel, London, 3rd November 2008
WENN Rights Ltd / Alamy Stock Photo

"It's 35 years since I joined Deep Purple and I look 18…"
Talking on Loose Women, UK TV, 16th April 2008

PNC Banks Arts Center, Holmdel, New Jersey, 11th July 2009
© Frank White Photo Agency

PNC Banks Arts Center, Holmdel, New Jersey, 11th July 2009
© Frank White Photo Agency

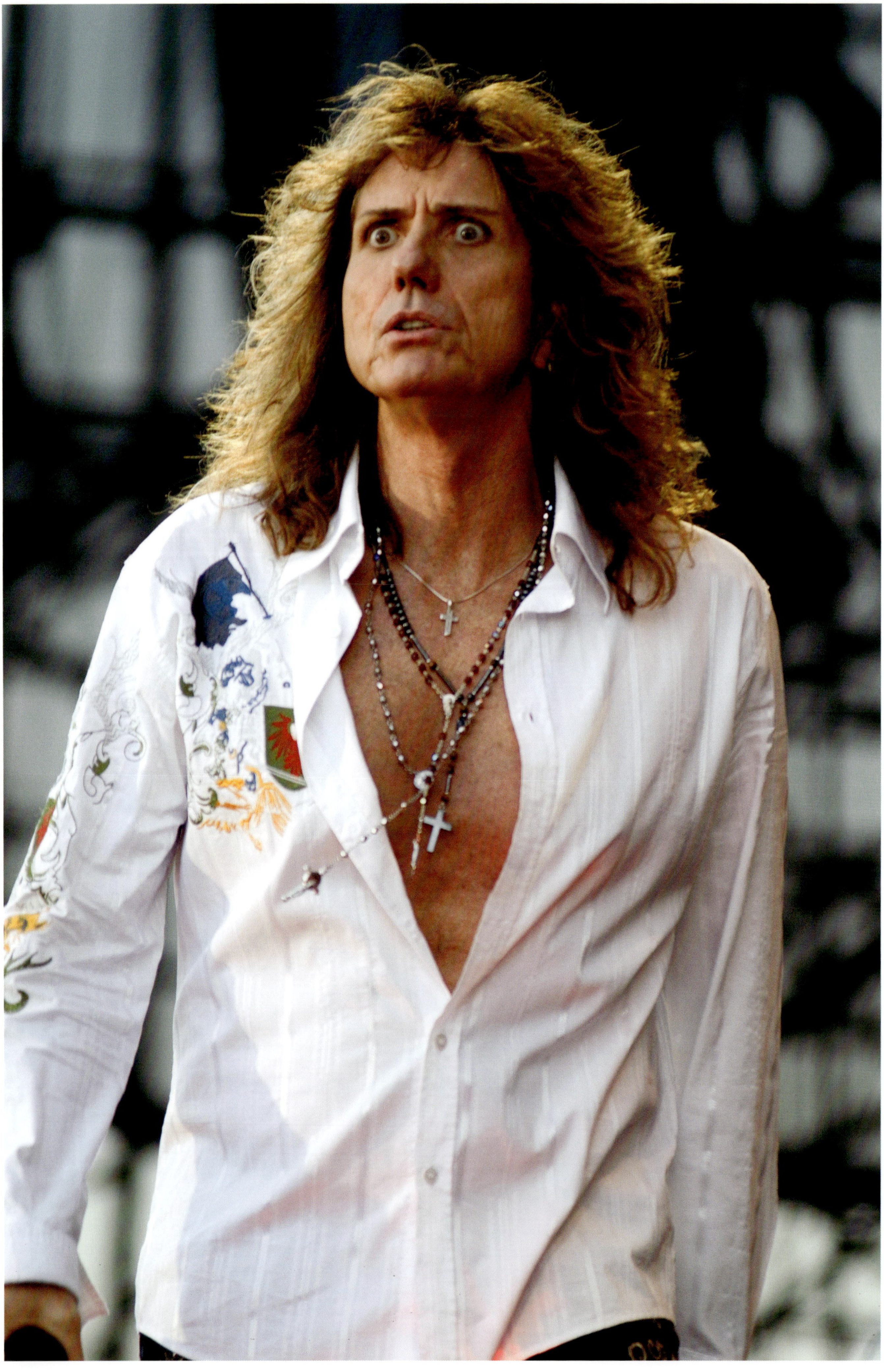

2009 At the Charter One Pavilion Chicago, Illinois, 19th July 2009. Whitesnake toured the States supporting Judas Priest's 'British Steel 30th Anniversary Tour 2009'.
(WENN Rights Ltd / Alamy Stock Photo)

"I'm a total drama queen and larger than life when away from my private life. When I go into that zone, it's David Coverdale amplified 10 or 11 times. That's not how I am at home. That's not how I am in my village. It's how I am when I'm inserted into this three-ring circus that we're all gainfully employed by."

2008 & 2009 were crammed with dates but from herein new albums have been produced at a more leisurely pace. 2011 delivered *Forevermore*, the second album that showcased David's writing partnership with Doug Aldrich.

"It's completely natural and inspiring to write with David. We have an unspoken trust that the other guy wants everything that is best for the song and the band. David and I have written so much that it feels like second nature. We start off with very basic ideas that we both seem excited about and then develop them into rough demos. Then obviously we record them with the entire band. We are always writing riffs and talking about song ideas. Then when I'm away, I try and achieve what David was describing. Or I try and get a vision that I have in my head in a very rough demo so I can pass it to David to have a think about." Doug Aldrich

With David in reflective mood he started to rebuild bridges with people from his past and the tour included guest appearances from former band members Adrian Vandenberg and Bernie Marsden.

Arriving at the 3rd Annual Revolver Golden Gods Awards Club Nokia, Los Angeles, California, 20th April 20 2011.
(The Photo Access / Alamy Stock Photo)

Hammersmith Apollo, London 20th June 2011
(WENN Rights Ltd / Alamy Stock Photo)

The death of Jon Lord in 2012 appeared to have an even more profound affect on David who clearly saw it was time to further bury the hatchet with past relationships that had soured and festered over the years.

" *The world is a lot worse off for his loss. I was so, so honoured to have known him and to have worked with him in two big bands. I can so easily visualise him right now. I remember bumping into him at a hotel a few years ago when he was on his way to Australia and we just sat down and had a drink together and the time just flew. It was so much fun to see him. Jon was extraordinarily articulate, charming and such a funny man. He was so gifted musically too and I totally miss him.*"

At The 3rd Annual Vegas Rocks! Magazine Awards at The Joint inside the Hard Rock Hotel and Casino, Las Vegas, Nevada 26th August 2012.
(James Atoa/Everett Collection/Alamy Live News)

With Doug Aldrich, his son Jasper and his wife Cindy Coverdale
(James Atoa/Everett Collection/Alamy Live News)

At the Multipurpose Fontes do Sar, Santiago de Compostela, Galiza, Spain, 28th June 2013 during the Year of The Snake Tour. (WENN Rights Ltd / Alamy Stock Photo)

Soon after Lord's death, David reached out to Ritchie Blackmore with the view to a possible collaboration. Although they had different visions as to what that might be and amicably continued on their separate paths, it certainly sowed the seed for the next Whitesnake album that surprised many fans.

In 2015 *The Purple Album* was a full-on nostalgia trip for David as Whitesnake revisited and re-recorded 15 Deep Purple songs. From May through to December the Purple Tour snaked its way across USA, Japan and Europe.

Casino Rama Toronto, Ontario, Canada. 2nd July, 2015.
(Igor Vidyashev/ZUMA Wire/Alamy Live News)

Mark Getess Arena, Trump Taj Mahal Casino,
Atlantic City, New Jersey, 25th July 2015
© Frank White Photo Agency

Mark Getess Arena,
Trump Taj Mahal Casino,
Atlantic City, New Jersey,
25th July 2015
© Frank White Photo Agency

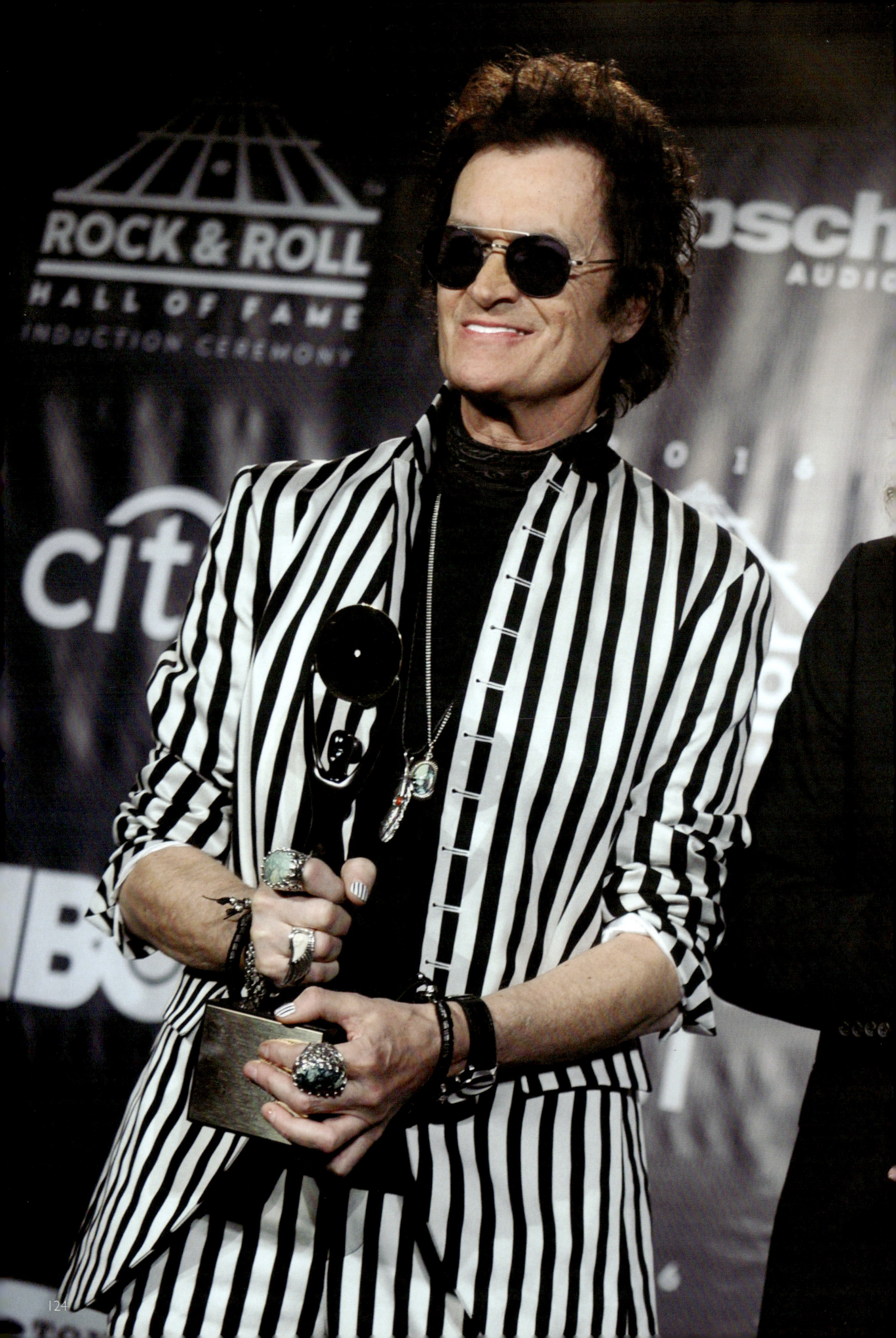
ROCK & ROLL
HALL OF FAME

Following the Purple Tour, Deep Purple was inducted into the Rock 'n' Roll Hall of Fame, which saw David receive his award alongside Glenn Hughes, Ian Paice, Roger Glover and Ian Gillan on 8th April 2016.

David and Glenn in the press room at the 31st Annual Rock And Roll Hall Of Fame Induction Ceremony at Barclays Center of Brooklyn, New York, 8th April 2016
(Storms Media Group / Alamy Stock Photo)

2016's touring was billed as the Greatest Hits Tour and included several shows in South America.

With Mick Jones of Foreigner at Live Nation's National Concert Week press day at Live Nation NYC Headquarters, 30th April 2018. Whitesnake, Foreigner and Jason Bonham commenced a three-act US tour in June of 2018, billed as the Juke Box Heroes Tour.
(Diego Corredor/Media Punch/Alamy Live News)

2018 should have seen the release of the most recent Whitesnake album but technical issues delayed it until May 2019. Although the band's popularity in the States isn't a patch on what it was in the late eighties, *Flesh And Blood* managed to reach the top 20 in ten countries, proving that David's decision to reactivate Whitesnake for the twenty-first century was fully vindicated.

The world pandemic of 2020/21 put pay to any touring but Coverdale's farewell tour under the Whitesnake name kicked off in May 2022.

What the future holds we will have to wait and see but David summed up the journey to date perfectly on 'Don't Fade Away':

> All in all it's been a rocky road,
> Twists and turns along the way
> But, I still pray for tomorrow,
> All my hopes, my dreams
> Don't fade away

Mark Getess Arena, Trump Taj Mahal Casino,
Atlantic City, New Jersey, 25th July 2015
© Frank White Photo Agency